Winnie-the-Pooh

Tigger is Unbounced

Adapted from the stories by A.A. Milne

One day Rabbit and Piglet were sitting outside Pooh's front door listening to Rabbit, and Pooh was sitting with them. It was a drowsy summer afternoon, so Pooh got into a comfortable position for not listening to Rabbit, and from time to time he opened his eyes to say "Ah!" and then closed them again to say "True," and from time to time Rabbit said, "You see what I mean, Piglet," very earnestly, and Piglet nodded earnestly to show that he did.

"In fact," said Rabbit, coming to the end of it at last, "Tigger's getting so Bouncy nowadays that it's time we taught him a lesson. Don't you think so, Piglet?"

Piglet said that Tigger was very Bouncy, and that if they could think of a way of unbouncing him it would be a Very Good Idea.

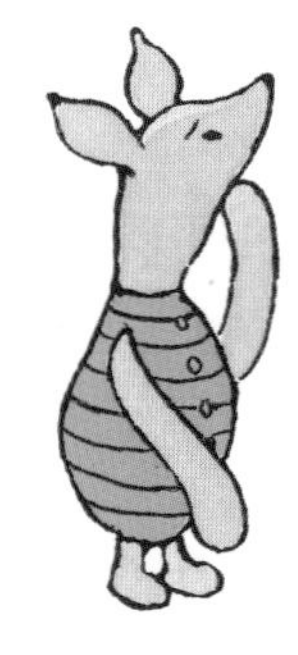

"Well, I've got an idea," said Rabbit, "and here it is. We take Tigger for a long explore, somewhere where he's never been, and we lose him there, and next morning we find him again, and – mark my words – he'll be a different Tigger altogether."

"Why?" said Pooh.

"Because he'll be a Humble Tigger. Because he'll be a Sad Tigger, a Melancholy Tigger, a Small and Sorry Tigger, an Oh-Rabbit-I-*am*-glad-to-see-you Tigger. That's why."

"I should hate him to go *on* being Sad," said Piglet doubtfully.

"Tiggers never go on being Sad," explained Rabbit. "They get over it with Astonishing Rapidity. But if we can make Tigger feel Small and Sad just for five minutes, we shall have done a good deed."

So it was arranged that they should start next morning.

The next day was quite a different day. Instead of being hot and sunny, it was cold and misty. But when Piglet and Pooh got to Rabbit's house, Rabbit said it was just the day for them, because Tigger always bounced on ahead of everybody, and as soon as he got out of sight, they would hurry away in the other direction, and he would never see them again.

"Not never?" said Piglet.

"Well, not until we find him again, Piglet. Tomorrow, or whenever it is. Come on. He's waiting for us."

When they got to Kanga's house, they found that Roo was waiting too, being a great friend of Tigger's, which made it Awkward; but Rabbit whispered "Leave this to me" behind his paw to Pooh, and went up to Kanga.

"I don't think Roo had better come," he said. "Not today."

"Why not?" said Roo, who wasn't supposed to be listening.

"Nasty cold day," said Rabbit, shaking his head. "And you were coughing this morning."

"Oh, Roo, you never told me," said Kanga reproachfully.

"It was a biscuit cough," said Roo, "not one you tell about."

"I think not today, dear. Another day."

So off they went, without Roo.

At first Pooh and Rabbit and Piglet walked together, and Tigger ran round them in circles, and then, when the path got narrower, Rabbit, Piglet and Pooh walked one after another, and Tigger ran up and down in front of them, and sometimes he bounced into Rabbit and sometimes he didn't.

And as they got higher, the mist got thicker, so that Tigger kept disappearing, and then when you thought he wasn't there, there he was again, saying, "I say, come on," and before you could say anything, there he wasn't.

Rabbit turned round and nudged Piglet.

"The next time," he said. "Tell Pooh."

"The next time," said Piglet to Pooh.

"The next what?" said Pooh to Piglet.

Tigger appeared suddenly, bounced into Rabbit, and disappeared again. "Now!" said Rabbit. He jumped into a hollow by the side of the path, and Pooh and Piglet jumped after him. They crouched in the bracken, listening.

The Forest was very silent when you stopped and listened to it. They could see nothing and hear nothing.

"H'sh!" said Rabbit.

"I am," said Pooh.

There was a pattering noise ... then silence again.

"Hallo!" said Tigger, and he sounded so close suddenly that Piglet would have jumped if Pooh hadn't accidentally been sitting on most of him.

"Where are you?" called Tigger.

"That's funny," said Tigger.

There was a moment's silence, and then they heard him pattering off again.

"Well?" Rabbit whispered proudly. "There we are! Just as I said."

And they all hurried off, Rabbit leading the way.

"Why are we going along here?" said Pooh, after a little while had passed.

"Because it's the way home," Rabbit said confidently.

"Oh!" said Pooh.

"I *think* it's more to the right," said Piglet nervously. "What do *you* think, Pooh?"

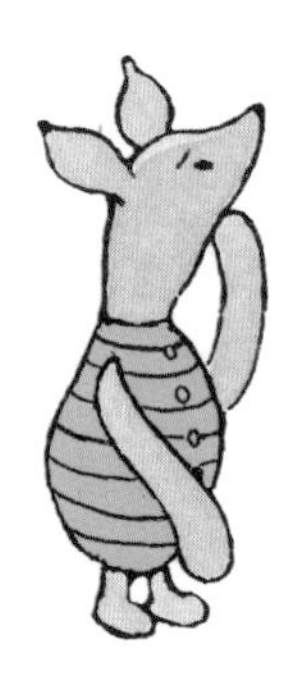

Pooh looked at his two paws. He knew that one of them was the right, and he knew that when you had decided which one of them was the right, then the other one was the left, but he never could remember how to begin.

"Well —" he said slowly.

"Come on," said Rabbit. "I know it's this way."

They went on. Ten minutes later they stopped again.

"It's a funny thing," said Rabbit, "how everything looks the same in a mist. Have you noticed it, Pooh?"

Pooh said that he had.

"Lucky we know the Forest so well, or we might get lost," said Rabbit half an hour later, and he gave the careless laugh which you give when you know the Forest so well that you can't get lost.

Piglet sidled up to Pooh from behind.

"Pooh!" he whispered.

"Yes, Piglet?"

"Nothing," said Piglet, taking Pooh's paw. "I just wanted to be sure of you."

When Tigger had finished waiting for the others to catch him up, he thought he would go home. So he trotted back; and the first thing Kanga said when she saw him was, "There's a good Tigger. You're just in time for your Strengthening Medicine," and she poured it out for him.

"Now then, run along," said Kanga.

"Where shall we run along to?" asked Roo.

"You can go and collect some fir-cones for me," said Kanga, giving them a basket.

So they went to the Six Pine Trees, and threw fir-cones at each other until they had forgotten what they came for, and they left the basket under the trees and went back to dinner. And it was just as they were finishing dinner that Christopher Robin put his head in at the door.

“Where’s Pooh?” he asked.
“Tigger dear, where’s Pooh?” said Kanga.

Tigger explained what had happened at the same time that Roo was explaining about his Biscuit Cough and Kanga was telling them not both to talk at once, so it was some time before Christopher Robin guessed that Pooh and Piglet and Rabbit were all lost in the mist on the top of the Forest.

"Well," said Christopher Robin, "we shall have to go and find them, that's all. Come on, Tigger."

* * * *

"The fact is," said Rabbit, "we've missed our way somehow."

They were having a rest in a small sand-pit on the top of the Forest. Pooh was getting rather tired of that sand-pit, and suspected it of following them about, because whichever direction they started in, they always ended up at it.

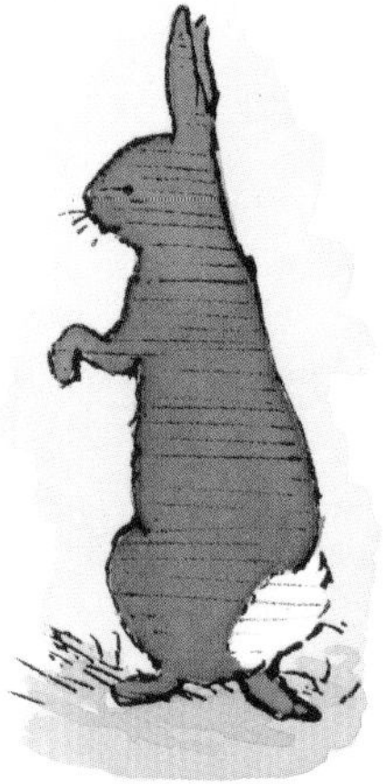

"Well," said Rabbit, after a long silence, "we'd better get on, I suppose. Which way shall we try?"

"How would it be?" said Pooh slowly, "if, as soon as we're out of sight of this Pit, we try to find it again?"

"What's the good of that?" said Rabbit. "If I walked away from this Pit, and then walked back to it, of *course* I should find it."

"Well, I thought perhaps you wouldn't," said Pooh. "I just thought."

"Try," said Piglet suddenly. "We'll wait here for you."

Rabbit gave a laugh to show how silly Piglet was, and walked into the mist. After he had gone a hundred yards, he turned and walked back again . . . and after Pooh and Piglet had waited twenty minutes for him, Pooh got up.

"I just thought," said Pooh. "Now then, Piglet, let's go home."

"But, Pooh," cried Piglet, all excited, "do you know the way?"

"No," said Pooh. "But there are twelve pots of honey in my cupboard, and they've been calling to me for hours. I couldn't hear them properly before because Rabbit *would* talk, but if nobody says anything except those twelve pots, I *think*, Piglet, I shall know where they're coming from. Come on."

They walked off together; and for a long time Piglet said nothing, so as not to interrupt the pots; and then suddenly he made a squeaky noise… and an oo-noise… because now he began to know where he was; but he still didn't dare to say so out loud, in case he wasn't. And just when he was getting so sure of himself that it didn't matter whether the pots went on calling or not, there was a shout from in front of them, and out of the mist came Christopher Robin.

"Oh, there you are," said Christopher Robin carelessly, trying to pretend that he hadn't been Anxious.

"Here we are," said Pooh.

"Where's Rabbit?"

"I don't know," said Pooh.

"Oh – well, I expect Tigger will find him. He's sort of looking for you all."

"Well," said Pooh, "I've got to go home for something, and so has Piglet, because we haven't had it yet, and —"

"I'll come and watch you," said Christopher Robin.

So he went home with Pooh, and watched him for quite a long time… and all the time he was watching, Tigger was tearing round the Forest making loud yapping noises for Rabbit. And at last a very Small and Sorry Rabbit heard him.

And the Small and Sorry Rabbit rushed through the mist at the noise, and it suddenly turned into Tigger; a Friendly Tigger, a Grand Tigger, a Large and Helpful Tigger, a Tigger who bounced, if he bounced at all, in just the beautiful way a Tigger ought to bounce.

"Oh, Tigger, I *am* glad to see you," cried Rabbit.